The Girl Who Loved Coyotes

The Girl Who Loved Coyotes

STORIES OF THE SOUTHWEST

BY **Nancy Wood**

ILLUSTRATIONS BY **Diana Bryer**

MORROW JUNIOR BOOKS
NEW YORK

For Ian, Bradford, Matthew, and Sydney,
whose young minds are open to ideas and imagination.
—N.W.

To all women who, like me, love coyotes.
—D. B.

Oil on linen was used for the full-color illustrations.
The text type is 12.25-point Giovanni Book.

Text copyright © 1995 by Nancy Wood
Illustrations copyright © 1995 by Diana Bryer

Printed in the United States of America.
1   2   3   4   5   6   7   8   9   10

Library of Congress Cataloging-in-Publication Data
The girl who loved coyotes: stories of the Southwest/by Nancy Wood;
illustrations by Diana Bryer.   p.   cm.
Contents: The girl who loved coyotes—Sun Mother and Moon Mother—How coyote got his song—The animal convention—How the coyotes lost their voices—The rainbow bridge—How the girl taught the coyotes to sing harmony—How eagle learned to see—How coyote married the girl—White buffalo girl—The coyote who became a star—The bear who courted the farmer's daughter.
ISBN 0-688-13981-7 (trade)—ISBN 0-688-13982-5 (library)
1. Tales—Southwest, New.   [1. Folklore—Southwest, New.]   I. Wood, Nancy C.
II. Bryer, Diana, ill.   PZ8.1.G456   1995   398.2'0979—dc20   95-9704   CIP   AC

CONTENTS

PREFACE

A Huge and Mystical Land

The great American Southwest is a huge, sun-drenched, and mystical land, larger than Spain and Portugal combined. The area includes New Mexico, Arizona, and northwest Texas, most of it high desert where less than ten inches of rain falls each year, except for islands of alpine growth along the widely scattered mountain ranges. Most of the landscape is barren, pale rose in color, crisscrossed with dry arroyos, where angry waters rush during flash floods in summer. The vegetation consists of cactus, sagebrush, chamisa, and low forests of piñon and juniper; along the arroyos lonely stands of cottonwood and Russian olive trees provide the only leafy green. This is a sparsely inhabited land, where fifteen generations of Hispanic farmers have wrested a living from the hard, alkaline soil, using *acequias*, or irrigation ditches, to water crops of corn, beans, squash, melons, chilies, and fruit. Today, this ancestral land is in great demand as homesites by a new wave of settlers from California and points east.

The Indian Way

The region's first farmers were called Anasazi, or the Old Ones. They came from the southwest about two thousand years ago, settling along river systems such as the Rio Grande, the San Juan, the Pecos, and the Gila. Their mystical and practical world was a balanced one, revolving around nature and all her seasons, creatures, and mystery. For long centuries, they lived in mud villages, migrating when drought, lack of game, or invasion by other tribes forced them out of their homelands. They recorded what they felt and saw in rock art, called petroglyphs; the essence of their complex belief system was handed down as myths, which are still repeated in the secret religious rituals of modern-day Pueblo Indians.

When Spanish explorers and priests arrived from Mexico, in 1540, they brought with them many strange things, the greatest of which was the horse. Indian culture changed dramatically. So did the art of storytelling, which up until then had revolved around wild animals, the deeds of warriors, the power of the kachinas (intermediaries between man and the spirit world), and the very cosmos itself. Now the factors of invasion and change were added, in addition to the secrecy needed to maintain the ancient Indian religion, practiced in underground ceremonial chambers called kivas. Thousands of Pueblo Indians were killed for cherishing their time-honored beliefs in defiance of the new Catholic regime. Priests also gave each male Indian a Spanish surname—Martinez, Lujan, or Tafoya, for instance—after their own last names. These are still used, in addition to a long string of tribal names known only to the Indians themselves.

How the Stories Came About

As intense conflicts raged between the two cultures, mainly over religious and land issues, stories arose out of mutual suffering and were told around tribal fires and in front of Spanish hearths alike. Each story had similar elements of danger, mystery, and help from the supernatural, though each was told in a different language, with a different idea of God at its center. From the late sixteenth to the early nineteenth century, New Mexico was controlled by land-hungry Spanish kings and authoritative popes, who lived an ocean away. Though settlement was continuous and the Indians were gradually subdued, the enormous land was frightening to the Spaniards, who made their first homes inside the high-walled pueblo villages, where they were safe from attack by warring tribes such as Navajos and Apaches. Frequent intermarriage between Spanish and Indian has taken place over the last four centuries, resulting in descendants who speak both the Indian and the Spanish languages, whose physical characteristics are a blend of both races, and whose stories often reflect a dual heritage.

Because of this common past, incongruities were, and still are, inevitable. While a priest says Mass in one of the Pueblo Indian mission churches, for instance, tribal members may be outside in the plaza, dancing to their ancient gods for rain. It has been so for four hundred years. A curious dichotomy is especially evident in Pueblo Indian religion, which was never wiped out despite persistent Catholic priests, harsh boarding schools, or vicious government raids on kivas. Today, every Pueblo village honors its ancient roots as well as its Catholic patron saints.

The American Connection

During the early years of settlement, New Mexico remained isolated from the outside world. Only Spanish and half a dozen native languages were spoken, and despite a major Indian revolt in 1680, during which all things Spanish were destroyed and Spanish priests and settlers were either killed or driven out, an uneasy harmony existed. When the great influx of non-Spanish people occurred after 1848, the New Mexicans referred to them generally as "gringos" and later as "anglos," a generic term that applied to all white-skinned people, regardless of their origin.

Gringos or anglos, the new wave of invaders brought with them a strong new cultural influence in terms of language, music, dance, art, architecture, food, and clothing. Soldiers, cowboys, trailblazers, railroad builders, fur trappers, and homesteaders came from the East with the expansionist ideals of the nineteenth century; these eventually disrupted Native American naturalism in every part of the North American continent. The vast expanses of mountains, semiarid plateaus, and remote valleys, and an almost primitive and superstitious mode of life, made New Mexico difficult to conquer; it was, and is, a last frontier where the presence of three distinct cultures is evident everywhere. While each culture fiercely holds on to its own individual identity, the tricultural aspect of New Mexico has produced a unique folklore.

Where Coyote Speaks the One True Language

A figure central to this folklore is Coyote, a wily, magical creature who is also a figure of legend among primitive peoples the world over. Coyote is the essence of both good and evil, a trickster and a wise teacher; he's been called the Imitator, the Old Man, and the First Creator. He is both God and man, human and subhuman; the Anasazi recognized him as a supernatural being thousands of years ago and dedicated a number of petroglyphs to his likeness. Coyote is truly the embodiment of the great Southwestern spirit, surviving against impossible odds. While he is the creation of primitive people, it is entirely natural that Coyote is also found in modern northern New Mexican folklore, in isolated villages with deep roots in the harsh land. There, Coyote speaks the one true language. It is one of experience, hard work, luck, and survival; in short, very much like the people themselves.

This book of twelve original stories is an attempt to introduce the reader to a mystical, enduring land, where it is said that sometimes coyotes can turn into people and people can fly away to the moon. Here, too, bears can fall in love with farmers' daughters, just as girls can teach coyotes to sing harmony. It's that kind of magical land.

THE GIRL WHO LOVED COYOTES

There was once a girl who lived high in the mountains with her family in a *casita* made of adobe. In the nearby forest were many animals, including coyotes who howled so loudly that people couldn't sleep. They said coyotes were a nuisance. Everyone except the girl hated coyotes. She rather liked their company from time to time. Their gentle faces soothed her.

Whenever she was watching her father's sheep, the girl sang *canciones* her grandmother had taught her. The animals listened—bears and deer, elk and porcupines, blue jays and tiny ants, even a curious mole who lived underground. All of them agreed: that girl had the most beautiful voice in the world. They gathered round to listen to her.

When the coyotes heard the girl singing, they too came out of the forest. They noticed how pretty she was, with hair the color of a raven's wing and eyes like bright stars. She didn't seem afraid of them, like so many people were. She told them to sit beside her.

"I'm tired of watching sheep," she complained. "They aren't very smart. They're always running away. They can't sing either."

One coyote moved closer. "Why not live with us, *amiguita*?" he said. "Then you won't have to watch those stupid sheep." But the girl was afraid to live with the coyotes. What would her *familia* say?

One evening when the girl was resting under a tree the coyotes came out of the forest and started to sing. When she sat up, she saw them standing in a circle, looking at her with concern in their eyes.

"¿*Cómo estás, amiguita*?" said the first coyote. "We've been thinking a lot about you lately. We wondered how you were."

"We're lonely, *amiguita*," said the second coyote. "We haven't been able to

sleep for many nights. You are always on our minds."

"We're afraid, *amiguita,*" said the third coyote. "People are trying to kill us." He showed the girl a metal trap on his hind leg.

The girl felt sorry for the coyote. Carefully, she removed the trap from his leg. She took water from the ditch and washed the wound. Then she tied her kerchief around it. When she was done, he licked her face. "You are so kind, *amiguita,*" he said. "*Gracias.*"

Meanwhile, the other coyotes killed an old sheep and started eating it. When the girl saw this, she cried, "*¡Alto!* Those are my father's sheep!" Unconcerned, the coyotes went right on eating. It was their first meal in a while.

"It's our nature to eat sheep," said one coyote who was feeling quite full. The girl burst into tears. She knew she'd be in trouble when her *padre* found out. She was supposed to be guarding those sheep!

As soon as the coyotes were finished eating, they began to sing again. Through her tears the girl sang with them. She didn't see her *padre* coming up the hill to find her. He went *muy loco* when he saw the remains of that old sheep. He yelled at the girl, then he ran to fetch his rifle to kill the coyotes. He was going to get rid of every single one.

The coyotes knew they didn't have much time. "We are your *amigos*," they said to the girl as they started to run. "We love you. Come with us, and you'll never be lonely. Come with us, and you'll never be hungry. Come with us, and we will make you happy."

The girl thought it over. She didn't want to spend her life watching sheep, and she certainly wanted to be happy, so she decided to run away with the coyotes. She lived with them ever after, and learned their coyote ways. People say that when the new moon rises and tries to catch the stars overhead, they hear the girl singing with those coyotes. Hers is the sweetest voice of all.

SUN MOTHER AND MOON MOTHER

A long time ago, before the earth was created, two sisters lived in darkness somewhere in deepest space. Thought Woman, the spirit who connects the universe, taught these *dos hermanas* language, music, and ways to survive. She gave them two baskets that contained all the seeds and bones of every plant and animal that was to be born in the coming world. In the darkness of the universe, the sisters planted the seeds of four pine trees. When one of the trees grew tall enough to pierce the darkness, they climbed out into light. They greeted the sun for the first time, offering it gifts of cornmeal and pollen. The Creator threw a ring of fire into space and *el mundo*, the world, was born.

The sisters went down to the cooling earth with their baskets, laying down seeds and bone. They threw pebbles in all directions and watched mountains and rivers form. They threw the first birds into the sky, and all but the turkey and the roadrunner took wing. Other creatures sprang forth from bone—deer, elk, bear, and buffalo. Turtles, snakes, and fish were placed where they belonged.

But the sisters were lonely. They wanted children. Thought Woman told them to lie down in the rain because in those days raindrops could become children. After the first rain, twins were born to each sister. The children were named Sky and Water, Fire and Corn. After that, one sister came to be called Sun Mother—*Madre Sol*—and she bore nothing but sons. The other sister came to be called Moon Mother—*Madre Luna*—and she bore nothing but daughters.

Their children married one another and went off in the four directions, all over the earth and across the oceans. They populated the world with all colors

and sizes of two-legged creatures. Blood and memory connect them to each of us, even to the present day.

HOW COYOTE
GOT HIS SONG

When Coyote first came into the world, he had no song. A funny sort of growl came out whenever he tried to sing. It sounded like he had a mouthful of stones rolling around on his tongue. Try as he might, he couldn't sing the way he wanted to. The other animals laughed. They said, "Listen to that stupid coyote gargling with a mouthful of stones. Too bad he doesn't have a song of his own as we do." Coyote sniffed. He didn't think those animals sang worth a darn.

Coyote went around *la tierra*, trying to find a song that suited him. He liked the bugling sound of the elk, but it was too loud for him. He liked the soft, sighing sound of the butterfly, but no one except Coyote could hear it. The sweet song of the meadowlark appealed to him, but the bird flew away before he could steal it.

Finally Coyote spotted a plain brown bird sitting in a tree. This bird wasn't much to look at, but as Coyote listened, she sang a beautiful song.

"Why, that's the meadowlark's song," Coyote said. In another moment the song had changed: now it was that of the mourning dove, now that of the bluebird, and all the songs were coming out of the same bird's throat! Coyote moved closer. "How can one bird sing so many songs?" he asked.

"Because I'm a mockingbird, silly," she said. "I can sing songs of any bird I happen to hear. I have my choice." Then she sang a wild canary song.

When she was finished, Coyote decided to impress her. "Now listen to *my* song," he said importantly.

Coyote fluffed up his fur and swung his tail and laid his ears back on his head. When he opened his mouth, the most terrible growl came out. Mockingbird laughed so hard she fell out of her tree. "You can't fool me," she said. "That's not a song. It's just loud noise."

"Very well," he said. "If you don't like my song, give me one of your own. You have so many, you'll never miss one little song."

Mockingbird started to sing another song, one that belonged to the warbler. Coyote liked this song best of all and wanted it for himself. "Give me that song," he said, moving closer. "Right now."

"Why should I give you a song?" Mockingbird said. "You're rude. You smell bad. Besides, animals aren't meant to sing like birds."

At that, Coyote pounced on poor Mockingbird, who had trusted him not to eat her. She had to think fast to save her life.

"All right. If I give you a song, will you let me go?" she asked, trying to sound brave. His sharp claws were hurting her.

When Coyote relaxed his grip, he saw that this plain brown bird might be useful. "What kind of song?" he asked hopefully. He closed one eye.

"Oh, one especially for you," Mockingbird said. She really didn't know any coyote songs, so she made one up. It went like this: *Ya-hoo-ooooh! Ya-hoo-ooooh!* or something very like it. That song echoed through the forest. "Now you try it," Mockingbird said. She'd never been able to trick a coyote before.

Coyote was so pleased with his song that he didn't notice it wasn't a bird-song at all. It was a new invention. He apologized to Mockingbird for being so rude, then he let her go. As she flew away, he opened his mouth. What came out made all the animals hide. It sounded like Coyote had a sore throat. He knew he sounded terrible, and he looked around for Mockingbird, but she was gone. *"Ya-hoo-ooooh!"* he went, over and over, until at last his voice improved.

Coyote took the song that Mockingbird gave him and practiced until he got it perfect. Now that he has a song all his own, the animals don't laugh at Coyote anymore. In fact, they say his is the best song of all because Mockingbird gave it to him, and it is the only song she ever gave to anyone. On the other hand, some animals say he might have stolen it, after all.

THE ANIMAL CONVENTION

When animals all spoke the same language in the early days of the world, things were peaceful until one day some two-legged creatures appeared. These creatures didn't have fur or feathers, just bare skin. Afraid of trouble, the animals gathered under the tree that was their favorite meeting place and held a convention. They were very worried.

Bear said: "I don't like the looks of those creatures. They're killing animals like us. They're wearing our hides for clothing." He tried to sink inside his thick fur.

Coyote said: "Don't worry. I can trick them into turning back the way they came from." But he wondered how to get their attention.

Eagle said: "I followed them across the mountains. They only take what they need. Perhaps they want to live in harmony with us."

Then Rabbit offered his view. "It looks like I'll be dinner for them," he said, and started to dig a hole to hide himself in. He had no wish to be eaten.

Deer was plenty worried too. Eagle had reported that the two-legged creatures especially liked the taste of roasted venison.

Mountain Lion said not to worry, he'd eat them. Bear said he'd scratch them to pieces. But Snake, who had slithered a long way to get there, had a solution. "Why don't we learn to live with them?" she suggested.

"I don't have to learn to live with anyone," Porcupine said crossly. "I'm content to live by myself. Nobody gets close to me." He raised the quills on his back; they were as sharp as needles.

"As for me," Squirrel chirped, "I can jump from tree to tree. I don't want to

learn to live with anybody either." And he launched himself into the next tree.

The animals began to worry about the end of their lives. They knew that the two-legged creatures had powers that they didn't have. As the two-legged creatures came closer, Bear looked up and gave them a name: "People!"

Ever since that convention, people have been the enemy of animals, who became aware that most humans meant to harm them.

HOW THE COYOTES LOST THEIR VOICES

Everyone knows how much coyotes love to sing all kinds of songs—one for play, another for danger, still others for hunting or making themselves known. Because they sing so much, all of the time, they sometimes lose their voices. This happened in a certain coyote village where those animals suddenly found themselves without voices. When they tried to sing, only croaks came out. They looked in the mountains, with the help of the bear; in the desert, with the help of the jackrabbit; even in the sky, with the help of the raven. The coyotes couldn't find their voices, no matter where they looked.

A girl who was their friend tried to help them, but nothing worked. Finally she decided to talk with the moon. *La luna* looked down and said: "Be at the horizon tomorrow night. I'll give you a ride in my lap. Then you'll be able to help your coyote friends."

The girl didn't know what the moon had in mind, but she started walking. She never reached the horizon because it kept moving away, as horizons do.

"If I can't get to the horizon," she sobbed as the moon began to rise, "how will I ever reach the moon?" Then the Great White Coyote, who had been following her, spoke up. "Jump," he commanded.

"But I'm afraid of heights," cried the girl. Looking at his strong back, she got an idea. "Will you come with me?" she asked.

"Certainly," said the Great White Coyote as he took her hand. They jumped as high as they could and caught the tail of the moon.

That night, when the coyotes looked at the moon there was the Great White Coyote! The face of the moon looked exactly like the face of the girl! Those coyotes were so shocked to see their friends up there in the sky that they found their voices at last. From that night on, they howled at the White Coyote and at the girl who stayed with him. If you listen carefully, you may even hear the girl and the White Coyote howling back at them, too. On some nights you may even see the White Coyote curled up on the moon, as big as life.

THE RAINBOW BRIDGE

In a certain part of the Southwest there is a deep, wide canyon, so big that you could put a city into it and no one would ever notice. One village lies on the south rim of this canyon, another village on the north. Because the canyon is so wide, it takes many days of riding a good horse to get from one side to the other. You have to go up and down the cliffs, over rocks, across a big river, and through many miles of forest.

A beautiful girl once lived along the south rim. She'd fallen in love with a boy from the north rim whom she'd met at a fair. She knew he loved her too, so she decided to visit him, but her parents said no. She dreamed of his handsome face, his merry eyes, and the way he rode a horse. I want to marry that boy, she said to herself. I will be miserable if I don't.

Over in his village, the boy was thinking about the girl every moment of the day. He wanted to visit her, but his parents said it was too far. All he could do was dream of her beautiful dark eyes and hair and how she dressed in a calico skirt and moccasins. He remembered the way she laughed and how stars twinkled in her eyes. She was the only girl he ever truly thought about.

So the girl and the boy only saw each other in their *sueños,* their dreams. They talked to each other on the wind, which carried messages back and forth, from his village to hers. Finally the girl decided to find the boy, no matter what her parents said. She called to him on *el viento,* telling him she was coming. It was a long way across, and she wondered what route to take. She couldn't climb down the steep, rocky walls of the canyon and pick her way through the wilderness. It was too dangerous. She got on her fine old *caballo,* who had been her friend since she was a little girl, and started riding along the rim, not sure of the way. She'd never traveled very far from home, and she was

frightened. Through cactus and forest she went, over slickrock and sagebrush. *Hacía mucho calor.* She rode on. When she got to the edge of the canyon, where it levels off, she looked ahead. There were still miles and miles to go. She was very tired and she had eaten all her food. In her canteen, she had only a few drops of water left. Far away, on the north rim of the canyon, she heard the boy calling to her on the wind. He said he was waiting. What was she to do?

All at once it started raining, hard enough that the girl got off her horse and sat under *un árbol* and waited for the storm to pass. When it did, she looked up and saw a rainbow stretching all the way from her side of the canyon to his! She clapped her hands with joy and mounted her horse. The rainbow looked like a bridge! She galloped toward it, the horse's hooves barely touching the ground. She wasn't even tired anymore.

The rainbow waited for the girl to come, trying to keep its colors as solid as it could. The rainbow became strong enough for the girl and the horse to ride across without falling through. When she slid off the rainbow at the other end, the boy was waiting. He took the girl in his arms and kissed her. She kissed him back.

"*Yo te quiero*," he said. "And I love the rainbow, too, for bringing you to me." They went to his village together, and there they were married. They were happy together, watching rainbows form.

Now, whenever young people see a rainbow in the sky, they wonder if it might be solid enough to ride a horse across. Then again, it might not hold them up at all. Maybe all a person needs is to believe that rainbows can turn into bridges, whenever someone really needs them to.

HOW THE GIRL TAUGHT THE COYOTES TO SING HARMONY

When coyotes first came into the world, they were bad singers. One sang high, another sang low. Another sang off-key. Too loud. Too soft. Too shrill. The other animals, who couldn't sing at all, called those coyotes a bunch of screech owls. "We're not screech owls," the coyotes said. "We're coyotes."

"Prove it," the other animals said, certain the coyotes would fail.

So the coyotes started out across the land to find a way to sing better. They sang on top of mountains. They sang in the middle of the desert. They sang in canyons. They were still bad singers. And the other animals were still making fun of them. What could they do? They talked among themselves, but none of them had an idea.

One day, as they were crossing an arroyo, they saw a girl playing her flute. The music sounded so appealing that they started to sing, very slowly and hesitantly at first. That flute could make coyote music! The girl noticed that the coyotes were singing along with it, even if they were off-key.

"Would you like me to teach you to sing harmony?" she asked.

The coyotes thought about it, then decided they had to learn. After all, they couldn't stand to have the other animals laughing at them. It was very hard work at first, but those coyotes tried to sound the way the flute did, not too sweet, not too sour, not too high, and not too low. They even tried to sing all together, on the same note and pitch. Night and day they sang. Through rain and snow they sang. Summer and winter they sang. Finally, they succeeded. When they did, the other animals stopped to listen. They were amazed at how beautiful the music was.

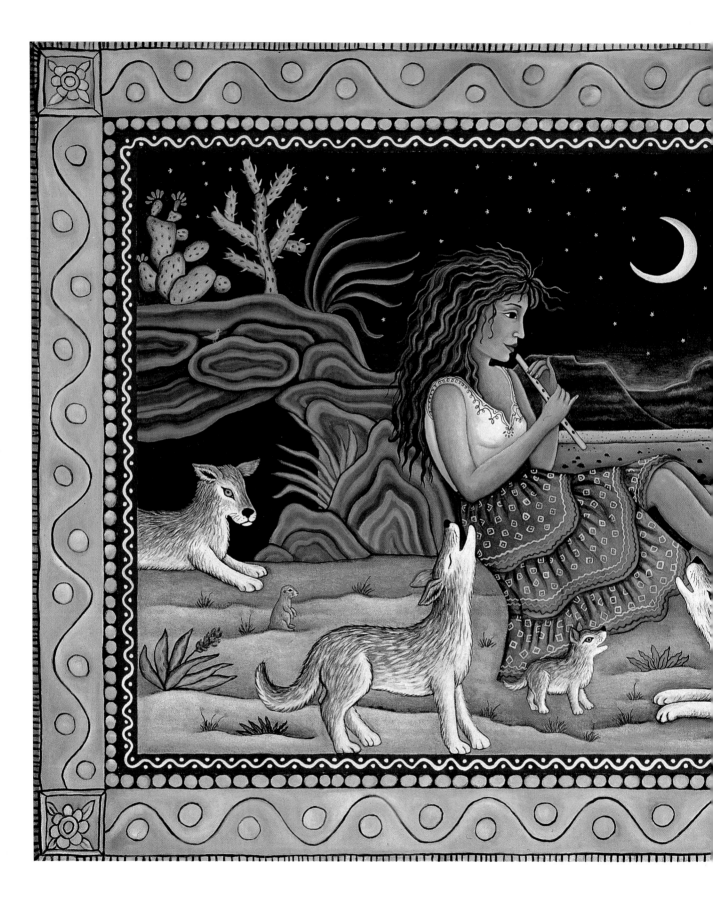

"Imagine that," they said, trying to sound like coyotes themselves, all those badgers, deer, bear, elk, and ground squirrels who can't sing at all. They began to respect the coyotes.

Now it's the coyotes who make the nighttime sweeter with their songs. Of course, the girl helps them stay in tune. The last time anyone looked, the girl and the coyotes were out in the middle of nowhere, practicing all night long.

HOW EAGLE LEARNED TO SEE

When he was first made by the Great Spirit, Eagle couldn't see very well. He had blurry vision, so the world looked fuzzy to him. He was always flying into things—trees and mountains and rocks, even clouds when he was soaring high. His beak turned out bent because he broke it flying into a cliff he couldn't see.

In those days there were no roads and no cities, no two-legged creatures and no loud noises. Just natural sounds of birds, wind, and rivers—also humming insects. Things were perfect then. But there was no one to bring the word about the earth's beauty from east to west, from north to south. The creatures who were on earth knew only about their own small places. They wondered what went on beyond the horizon. Stories brought back by turtles or bears or crows only went so far. Eagle could fly farther and faster than any other bird. The trouble was, he couldn't see well enough to be able to tell a bear from a pine tree.

One day the Great Spirit took Eagle aside and said: "If you can capture fire, Brother Eagle, I'll make you see better." Eagle wondered how he was supposed to do that without burning up, but the Great Spirit wouldn't tell him. "Find out for yourself," the Great Spirit said. "Why do you think I gave you a brain?"

Eagle thought and thought, but he couldn't figure out a way to capture fire, no matter how hard he tried. He was certain he'd always have poor vision and a beak that was permanently bent.

One stormy summer day, when Eagle was sitting on his ledge, trying to see what was happening below, lightning forked all across the sky. Eagle looked up. To him, lightning looked like a great golden river in the sky. Because he knew that rivers had fish, which he very much liked to eat, he decided that lightning probably was full of fish too. So off he went, trying to find fish swimming in the sky.

Back and forth Eagle went, up and down, this way and that, chasing lightning. Thunder rolled in every direction, and the sun hid its blazing face in dark clouds. But every time lightning flashed, Eagle was somewhere else. He wore himself out chasing lightning through the sky. So he went home to his ledge to rest. While he was sitting there—*ka-boom!*—lightning struck the ledge. It struck poor Eagle right in the mouth too. It wouldn't let go. He was sad to find out that lightning didn't contain fish at all. And it gave him a hot, tingling pain.

Eagle took off with lightning in his beak. He flew all over, trying to get rid of it. Bit by bit, he was able to drop pieces of lightning in trees or in fields of grass. Looking down, Eagle saw orange light springing up wherever he dropped lightning. And there was flame and smoke. When there was no more lightning left, Eagle flew home. As he fell asleep, he heard the Great Spirit say, "Thank you, Brother Eagle, for capturing fire. You proved it could be done."

Next morning, when Eagle awoke, he couldn't believe he could actually see far beyond the horizon! Mountain ranges that nobody in his family had ever seen before! A distant river filled with fish. Even little mice scurrying around, trying not to get caught. *Whoosh,* Eagle flew down and grabbed one. Then another. After his meal, he flew into the clouds and didn't bump into them the way he had before. Now he could see better than any bird in the sky.

From then on, Eagle's job was to fly to distant places and remember details to tell the other animals. The delicate wings of a butterfly. The tiny parts of flowers. Footprints of mice. Cones on a pine tree. The secret place where the rainbow ends. Eagle learned to see things so well that he saw them before they were born.

Even today, if you look very hard, you might see Eagle streaking across the sky with lightning in his beak, which is still as bent as it ever was. Some things are just meant to be that way.

HOW COYOTE
MARRIED THE GIRL

There was once a coyote who fell in love with a beautiful girl. The moment he saw her he was certain his heart would jump right out of his skin. She wore moonlight in her hair and the wind sang a special song for her. The girl noticed everything around her, but she didn't notice *him*, Coyote. "That girl doesn't notice me because she thinks I'm just an animal," Coyote said. "I'll show her what I really am." He spent hours trying to make himself presentable.

When the moon rose over the mountains, Coyote began to sing a love song. He put his heart into it, hoping she'd notice him at last. Finally the girl came to the door and saw poor Coyote standing on a rock, his head pointed up at the moon. She wasn't too impressed.

"*Buenas noches, Señor Coyote,*" she said, and shut the door. She didn't seem to care for him at all. Couldn't she see how he felt? Why, his heart was nearly broken in two.

Unhappy Coyote talked to his family about his love for the girl. One coyote said, "If you love her, you'll have to become a *muchacho*. It's the only way to make her notice you." Coyote agreed, though he much preferred to stay as he was.

Because he had magical powers, he was able to cast a spell on the girl when she fell asleep. When she awoke, she thought Coyote was a *muchacho*. How handsome he was! And how well he could sing all her favorite songs! Coyote even stayed around to help her with her chores, carrying wood for the fire and water from the *acequia*. The closer he got, the more he loved that girl.

Now, Coyote couldn't keep the girl under his spell forever. When the sun

went down, the spell wore off and she saw he was really a coyote. At first she was afraid, but then she remembered his songs and the way he'd helped with her chores. She didn't care what he was! She loved him anyway. When Coyote asked her to marry him, she accepted. Now she lives with him in a cave where coyotes and children play together because, in that special world, they are the best of friends.

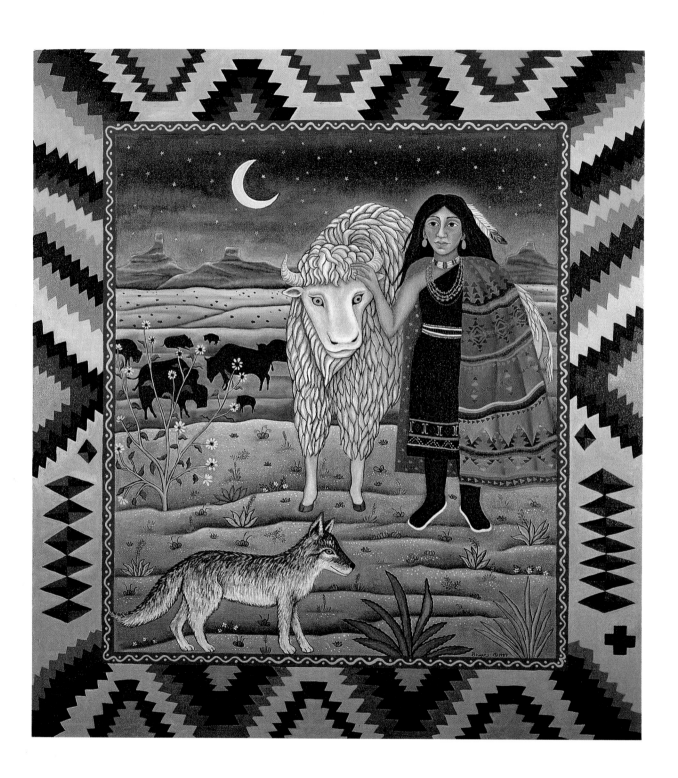

WHITE BUFFALO GIRL

In the old days, the Pueblo Indians used to ride out from their villages to hunt buffalo on the plains. They drove the herds through mountain passes back to their own lands, where they killed them. They used the meat for food and the hides for clothing. Nothing went to waste, not even bones.

When settlers started pushing across the plains, the railroads followed and the buffalo disappeared. Men shot them from railroad cars for the fun of it alone. They never ate the meat or used the hides. At about the same time, the Indians were rounded up and sent to reservations. The Pueblo Indians had most of their lands taken away.

One thing the white men didn't kill was the sacred White Buffalo. The Indians still saw him in their dreams, and he told them the buffalo would someday return. One warrior rode out from a reservation where the government had sent his people. When he came back, he said he couldn't find any buffalo, though he'd searched for days. More hearts were broken. The Indians thought the white man had killed them all. They didn't know that one herd had managed to run away and hide, deep in a remote valley.

After a while, a beautiful Indian girl appeared to the people of that tribe. She'd brought the sacred White Buffalo with her. He was standing there, big as life. He opened his mouth and said: "Come look. The buffalo have started to come back. Soon they will cover the land, same as before. The white man didn't kill them, after all."

The Indians ran outside and looked. Sure enough, there were plenty of buffalo, roaming around the plains the way they had before. The Indians held a big dance to thank the White Buffalo Girl. Because the spirit of the buffalo came back to them, they knew it was possible to survive anything, even life on the reservation and the death of their old ways.

THE COYOTE WHO
BECAME A STAR

There was once a coyote with *ojos amarillos*—yellow eyes—who was smarter than the rest. He was able to speak the language of trees, rocks, birds, and even people. The trouble was, because those yellow eyes made him look different, this coyote didn't have many friends. He traveled far and wide, seeking the right companion. He met a girl coyote that he liked, but she didn't like him. Then he met a bear who liked him, but the coyote didn't want to sleep all winter in a cave. Once, when he was in a forest, a blue jay rode on the coyote's back for many miles, but then he had to go home. Those were the only friends the coyote had.

As the lonely coyote traveled around, his companions were *el sol* and *la luna* and all the many *estrellas* glittering in the sky. The coyote was happy to have these *amigos* to talk to. "Come live with us," they said, but he was afraid to leave the earth he knew. Besides, he'd just found a coyote village that had welcomed him. They said he could stay as long as he liked. He was happy there, swapping stories with his coyote *amigos*. Eventually he hoped to settle down with them.

One day during a rainstorm the coyote was going along the banks of a river when he slipped and fell in. When he yelled for someone to help him, a badger tried to pull him from the water, but the coyote was too heavy. Then a bear jumped in to save him, but the coyote was swept over a waterfall. The animals watched helplessly as the coyote floated away. *"Adiós, amigos,"* he cried as muddy water covered his head.

So the poor coyote drowned. But because he'd been such a good friend, the stars came down and got him. They lifted him up to the waiting sky. Now, on certain nights of the year you can see the Coyote Star twinkling not far from the moon. People call it Canis Major, the Dog Star, but coyotes know better. They know a coyote when they see one.

THE BEAR WHO COURTED THE FARMER'S DAUGHTER

One spring the youngest bear in a family of bears woke up early, when the ice on the stream below began to break. He got up from his bed of leaves and stood at the mouth of the cave, looking out. The forest stretched on for many miles; the sky was so blue it hurt his eyes. As he watched, an eagle dipped his wings in greeting. Two beavers, busy chewing down aspen trees to make a dam, called to him as he climbed down the slope. *"Hermano Oso*, where are you going?"

As he plunged into the cold stream to take a bath, Bear said, "South to court a farmer's daughter." Something in his blood made Bear know it was time to take a wife. The summer before, when his father had taken him south to show him *El Río Grande*, a girl had waved to him as he passed by. He liked the look of her, so soft and pretty.

The beavers stopped chewing on the aspen trees and stared at him in amazement. "You're crazy, *Hermano Oso,*" they said. "People are afraid of bears. They'll shoot you the moment they see you."

"Nonsense," said Bear confidently. "No one will shoot me. I'll tell them stories of how the world used to be. Stories always make people gentle. Especially that girl I'm going to marry." At this, the beavers started to laugh. They knew that nothing made people gentle. Long ago many of their kind had been killed and made into beaver hats.

When he was finished with his bath, Bear looked at his reflection in the water. As bears go, he was rather handsome, with long white teeth and glossy black eyes and thick, soft fur. His ears were nicely rounded and he had a long, kind face. After he shook himself dry, Bear went down the mountain. He had a long way to go.

On her father's farm along *El Río Grande,* the girl was thinking about the bear she'd seen the year before. She'd noticed his kind expression, the way he stopped to look at her, and how there seemed to be great intelligence in his eyes. She hadn't been afraid of him then, the way some people were. She wasn't afraid as she thought of him now, wondering if he'd come to see her again. Just in case Bear decided to pay a visit, she went into her father's orchard and picked a basketful of ripe cherries. She waited for several days and was about to give up when she saw Bear's big, furry form running along the *acequia.*

"*Buenos días, muchacha,*" Bear said breathlessly. "I've come to tell you a story." This was how he hoped to capture her heart.

"*Buenos días, oso,*" the girl said. "I love stories." She offered him the cherries, which he ate hungrily.

When he was finished he sat down and took her small hands in his big paws. He drew in his deep bear breath and made a growling sound, but the girl didn't mind. "In the old days, only animals and birds lived here," he said. "People hadn't come along to ruin things. There was nothing but mountains and rivers and big sky as far as you could see. Imagine."

The girl closed her eyes. She imagined the peaceful way it had been, without fences or houses, roads or people. She settled herself in Bear's lap. "Tell me more," she said. So he did, from that day onward.

Every night, while they grew old together, Bear told stories to the farmer's daughter. By that time she'd gone to the mountains to live with him because she didn't want to miss a single bear story. In that way she acquired wisdom, which was Bear's true nature.

The girl's love made Bear happy. He'd spend winters lying near her, dreaming of spring, when she'd gather cherries for him again. Cherries reminded him of his youth, when all he had on his mind was courting a pretty girl with what was best and truest in his *corazón*.

GLOSSARY

Author's note: The limited use of Spanish words and phrases in this book is meant to add flavor to the stories. (You'll see that Spanish words often have both male and female spellings. When referring to a man or boy, a word ends in "-o"; when referring to a woman or girl, a word ends in "-a.") To learn more, readers are urged to consult bilingual works or to learn the Spanish language in their schools.

acequia   irrigation ditch
adiós   good-bye
alto   stop
amigo   friend
amiguita   little friend
buenas noches   good evening
buenos días   good day
caballo   horse
canción   song
casita   little house
¿cómo estás?   how are you?
corazón   heart
dos hermanas   two sisters
el mundo   the world
El Río Grande
    the Big River, which flows from
    Colorado down through New Mexico
    and forms the border between Texas
    and Mexico
el sol   the sun

el viento   the wind
estrella   star
familia   family
gracias   thanks
hacía mucho calor   it was very hot
hermano   brother
la luna   the moon
la tierra   the earth, the land
Madre Sol   Sun Mother
Madre Luna   Moon Mother
muchacha   girl
muchacho   boy
muy loco   very crazy
ojos amarillos   yellow eyes
oso   bear
padre   father
señor   mister
sueño   dream
un árbol   a tree
yo te quiero   I love you